PUFFIN

MOVE OVER

Margaret Springer was born near Croydon, Surrey in 1941 and moved to Canada with her family at the age of 11. After graduation from McGill University she worked in a social agency and as a librarian before becoming a full-time writer in 1982. Her stories, articles and poems for children have been widely published in Canada and the United States. She enjoys crafts, movies and plays, reading, music, walks and small furry creatures, and has been owned by pets including rabbits, cats and one opinionated monkey. Most of all she likes to write, or help others with writing. She has two grown-up children and now lives in Waterloo, Ontario, Canada.

SURFERS

MOVE OVER, EINSTEIN!

Margaret Springer

Illustrated by
Biz Hull

PUFFIN BOOKS

PUFFIN BOOKS

Published by the Penguin Group
Penguin Books Ltd, 27 Wrights Lane, London W8 5TZ, England
Penguin Books USA Inc., 375 Hudson Street, New York, New York 10014, USA
Penguin Books Australia Ltd, Ringwood, Victoria, Australia
Penguin Books Canada Ltd, 10 Alcorn Avenue, Toronto, Ontario, Canada M4V 3B2
Penguin Books (NZ) Ltd, 182–190 Wairau Road, Auckland 10, New Zealand

Penguin Books Ltd, Registered Offices: Harmondsworth, Middlesex, England

First published 1997
5 7 9 10 8 6 4

Text copyright © Margaret Springer, 1997
Illustrations copyright © Biz Hull, 1997

The moral right of the author and illustrator has been asserted

All rights reserved. Without limiting the rights under copyright reserved above,
no part of this publication may be reproduced, stored in or introduced into a retrieval
system, or transmitted, in any form or by any means (electronic, mechanical, photocopying, recording or otherwise), without the prior written permission of both the copyright owner and the above publisher of this book

Filmset in Bembo

Printed in England by Clays Ltd, St Ives plc

A CIP catalogue record for this book is available from the British Library

ISBN 0-14-37799-9

Contents

1	Tatty Kumpf, Scientist	1
2	The Biscuit Project	13
3	No Turning Back	25
4	A Closer Look	36
5	That William!	48
6	Cold Comfort	61
7	It's Not Fair!	74
8	Countdown	86
9	All in Pieces	98
10	Watch Out, World!	109

Chapter One
Tatty Kumpf, Scientist

TATIANA KUMPF AND her best friend Nicola Jenson trudged home through the snow and wind together.

"Isn't this weather horrible?" Tatiana hunched her shoulders as she ploughed her chunky frame forward.

Nicola nodded. "My dad said it's the worst winter he can remember."

The wind whipped the snow in gusts and blurred the pavement in front of them.

"Nicola! Tatty!" The voice went louder and softer as the wind blew it. The girls stopped, shielding their faces with mittened hands as they turned to look.

William McNair was leaping through the snow towards them. His red parka was a colourful blob in the whiteness, and as usual he was grinning. "I thought you'd never hear me," he said. "I've been yelling for ages. Did you see the notice, Tatty?"

"William," said Tatiana, "I've told you a million times not to call me Tatty. My name is Tatiana."

"I know, I know, but Tatty's quicker. Are you going to enter?"

"Enter what?"

"The Science Fair. Didn't you see the notice?"

"No." Tatiana thought back to science class. Mr P had given them a surprise test, and she knew everything except the last question – what do a whale, a shrew, a bat and a polar bear have in common? It took her ages to work out that they're all mammals. William finished early. He always had time for notice boards.

"Can anyone enter?"

"Of course. It's in February. I thought you'd be interested."

"A whole month away," said Nicola.

"There's prizes," William said. "Twenty-five pounds, from Trentner's Pharmacy. *And* – listen to this, Tatty – the winner from each school gets to go to the 'Young

Scientist' programme. You know, the one at the University?"

Tatiana knew. Going there was something she had always dreamed of. But it would cost money to enter. You'd need supplies, and things for your display.

"You'd have a good chance," said Nicola. "You're such a science nut. If you got it finished, that is."

"Of course I'd get it finished." Secretly Tatiana knew what Nicola meant. How many times had she started something and then, for one reason or another, given up on it? But those times, there was a good reason.

They had come to the place where a row of houses changed to a block of flats. William lived in the last house, Tatiana lived in the flats next door, and Nicola's bungalow was farther along, on a side road.

"Off I go," said William. "How do you like my snow machine?" He zig-zagged into his snowy driveway and made a loud motor noise, thrashing about with his arms and legs. "Bye, Nicola! Bye, Tatty!"

Nicola giggled. "He must be soaked."

But Tatiana was not smiling. "He called me Tatty again," she said. "And he gets higher marks than me, without any effort at all. How can anyone that messy be so smart?"

The wind whipped at them sideways and stung their faces. Tatiana hiked up her scarf one more time as they headed for her flat. She tried to imagine being in a real university lab, helping real scientists do their work. The competition would be tough. Could she really do it?

"I'll enter, Nicola," Tatiana said, as they stamped the snow off their boots in the hallway. "I'll enter. And I'll win, too."

Mum was ready for them, with two steaming mugs of cocoa and a plate of biscuits.

"I can't stay long today, Mrs Kumpf," Nicola said. "Today's my ballet."

"Of course, dear. Isn't it terrible out? Worst winter in years. I was afraid they'd cancel the buses and I wouldn't be able to get home." She arranged mitts and scarves over radiators. "How will you get to your ballet?"

"My mum drives me. Our van can get through anything."

"That's nice." Mum did a sort of pirouette. She was slim and graceful, like Nicola. "I always loved ballet, too. Did I tell you I once had a part in a toilet-paper commercial? I was the snowy-soft fairy. It showed about thirteen times that season."

"You've told her lots of times, Mother," said Tatiana.

"I always hoped Tatiana would take it up some day."

"I'm not going to," Tatiana said.

Mum sighed. "Well, it would be good for you." She bustled off into the bedroom.

Tatiana frowned after her. "She's always trying to get me to lose weight," she mumbled.

"You're not fat," said Nicola.

"No, but I'm not skinny like you."

The girls sipped their cocoa and warmed their hands on their mugs in silence.

"Do you really think I have a chance, Nicola? With the Science Fair?"

"Of course you do." Nicola smiled. "You always get good marks in science, sometimes even better than William. And you do a neater job than he does."

"I wouldn't even try if William was going in for it. He'd win without even trying." Tatiana gazed out of the window. She'd have to chose something difficult, and do it well. Chemistry, perhaps. Something to do with chemistry. But where –

"I'd better go." Nicola gathered her half-dry things.

"All right."

Long after the front door downstairs banged, Tatiana stared into her empty mug, thinking.

Mum appeared with newly mended clothes. "Your father seems to split the seams on every pair of trousers he buys," she said.

"He could stand to lose some weight, too."

"Mum, I'm not a blimp."

"I didn't say you were."

Tatiana decided to change the subject. "Do we have any science books?"

"The encyclopedia. What do you want to know about?"

"Chemistry. I've read about it in the encyclopedia."

Mum smiled. "Chemistry! Really, Tatiana, I wish you'd get interested in something more practical."

"Science is the most practical thing there is," flared Tatiana.

"I took the hem down on this skirt of yours. Now maybe you'll wear it more often. It's a pretty one."

Tatiana put her mug on the table. "I'm going to enter the School Science Fair next month, Mum. But I'll need money. There's prizes, and if you win, you get –"

"Is it a school event?"

"Yes. And the winner from each school gets to –"

"Then the school should be paying for it. It's not fair to charge an entry fee."

"It isn't an entry fee. It's for supplies and stuff, and –"

"Tatiana, remember the kite contest? We gave you the money to buy that expensive parachute material that's now in pieces, gathering dust in your room somewhere?"

"But that was different. I couldn't enter a kite that wouldn't fly. There was something wrong with my design and I didn't know how to fix it."

Mum sighed. "Tatiana, you know how

tight things are for us at the moment. We don't have much extra. You'll have to be more careful how you spend your allowance."

"You'd find money for ballet lessons."

"Ballet lessons are different."

There was a silence, except for a distant sweeping sound. William was clearing the paths next door.

"Why did you name me Tatiana?"

Mum looked startled. "Because it's a lovely name. You were our first daughter, our only daughter. You know that – you came ten years after the last of three boys –"

"I know, but why Tatiana?"

"Because it's a lovely name."

"Well, I don't like it. It sounds frilly and fancy. I hate it, in fact."

"Tatiana!"

"And I hate my other name, too. Kumpf! What sort of a silly name is that?"

"It's your great-grandfather's name, young lady, and you should be proud of it. He came to this country with nothing in nineteen twenty-five, and —"

"I know, I know. I'm sorry, Mum." Tatiana picked up her newly warmed mitts and scarf. "I'm going to the library."

"In this weather?"

"Yes. The sooner I start on my project the better. Whether anyone else cares or not."

She stomped out of the flat, down the stairs, and outside into the cold.

"I'm not a quitter," Tatiana muttered. "I do finish things."

She tried hard to believe it. Just this once.

Chapter Two
The Biscuit Project

"TATIANA KUMPF, DO you ever listen to me?"

Nicola was staring across the lunch table at Tatiana. She had been saying something, but what?

"I've been telling you about the try-outs

for my ballet recital, and you didn't hear one word I said."

"Sorry," Tatiana mumbled.

"You always get like this when you're on about something. It's the Science Fair, isn't it?"

Tatiana nodded. "I can't help it. I'm trying to come up with a good topic. I've got loads of ideas, but none of them are any good."

"You'll think of something."

"I'm going to win this one, remember. I want to be a scientist. I don't want to end up working in an office somewhere or selling dresses for the rest of my life."

"Hello!" Amy Jenson had manoeuvred her wheelchair into place beside them, shoving past obstacles with her usual determination. Amy's hair was short, and her face was rounder than Nicola's, but anyone could see they were sisters.

"We didn't hear you coming," said Nicola. "Shows how noisy this place is."

Tatiana reached to make room as Amy wedged herself in.

"I can manage," Amy said.

By now everyone in school was used to the hum of Amy's wheelchair as she buzzed about, usually at high speed. She was only a year older than Nicola, but already she was a maths whiz, and she knew more about computers than Tatiana and Nicola put together.

"I saw your dad the other day, Tatiana," Amy said. "When we went to buy shoes. I didn't know he worked at the Superstore."

Tatiana nodded. "He's only been there a few months," she said. Nicola knew that Dad had been laid off with the others at his old job. It wasn't something Amy had to know.

Amy jabbed a straw into her milk carton. "Does your mum work there, too?"

"No, she's in the fashion business."

Nicola's eyes widened, but she didn't say anything.

Well, it's true, thought Tatiana. An elastics factory is sort of fashion.

"Tatiana's entering the Science Fair, Amy," Nicola said. "She's going to win, too."

Amy looked at Tatiana. "Yeah? What are you doing it on?"

"I haven't decided yet."

"Really?" Amy seemed surprised. "Some year I'll enter, when I'm not so busy with Computer Club. I've already got my topic: computer security. You know, so people can't steal software or copy things they're not supposed to?"

"It costs money to enter," Nicola said.

"That's OK," said Amy. "Dad would give me the disks and stuff. I guess that's more of a problem for you, though, Tatiana?"

Tatiana was finishing the last of her lunch, a biscuit that tasted like thick cardboard with dried-up jam on it.

"Not really," she lied. "I've got that figured out."

"Oh?" said Nicola. "What have you decided?"

There was a pause. Tatiana swallowed the last bite of biscuit, then looked straight at Amy. "I'm going to have a biscuit sale here on Friday," she blurted out. "I'll sell good, home-made biscuits. That'll raise the money I need."

"I thought you hated cooking."

"It's – not so bad." Tatiana thought fast.

"It's – just chemistry. You have your formula, that's the recipe, and you mix things up and heat them so there's a chemical reaction between the ingredients –"

"Sounds gross," said Amy.

"I'll help," said Nicola.

Tatiana shook her head. "I can bake them myself. And I'll sell them myself, too. It's my project."

The school bell rang, a loud honking buzzer that shook the air and brought everyone to their feet, stampeding towards the lunchroom door.

"I've got good recipes," said Nicola. Amy had already streaked past them, disappearing into the crowd.

"I don't need recipes," said Tatiana. "I'll do it myself, all right?"

"All right!" Nicola turned away sharply

and walked quickly from Tatiana, pulling herself up to her full graceful height.

The crowd pushed past, but Tatiana stood for a moment.

Why did I do that? she wondered. Now Nicola's mad at me, and I'm having a biscuit sale in two days' time. I've never baked a decent batch of biscuits in my whole life.

Tatiana walked home alone that day. It was still very cold, though no longer snowing. At home, she pulled out the cookbooks.

"What are you working on?" Mum asked.

"I want to make biscuits."

"How nice! I didn't think you were interested –"

"I'm not." Tatiana frowned. "Well, I am, but it's homework, sort of. A fund-raising project."

"It's a long time since I made biscuits

myself. That was one thing I had to give up when I went back to work." Mum put aside her embroidery.

"It's OK," said Tatiana. "I can do it. I'll pay you back for the stuff I use."

"You don't need to do that, dear. I won't notice a bit of flour missing."

"You'll notice this. I'm going to make about two hundred."

"Two hundred! When are you going to do this?"

"Tomorrow evening, Thursday. Then they'll be fresh for the sale on Friday."

"I won't be able to help you. Thursday's my choir night."

"I know that." Tatiana was glad it worked out that way. "I can manage."

The next day she often glanced across the

classroom at Nicola, or noticed Nicola looking at her. But they didn't speak to each other. Not once.

After school Tatiana headed for the supermarket with her list. Flour. Chocolate chips. Raisins. Spices. So much to buy.

She stopped to add it all up. This was ridiculous. Maybe I'll forget the whole thing, Tatiana decided. But I can't. I need the money, and I got permission at school to hold the sale, and I put up signs.

And if I cancel now, I'll have to explain things to Amy, and I'll be a quitter again.

Her trolley lurched sideways and she yanked it back irritably. A display caught her eye. Biscuit mix. Just add water.

"Hey!" Tatiana said out loud. "Just because they're home-made doesn't mean they have to be from scratch." She grabbed four packets and raced back down the aisle.

That evening as soon as Mum left for choir, Tatiana lined everything up on the kitchen counter.

Dad was in the living room, watching football on television. "You need help?" he called.

"No thanks," said Tatiana. "I'll shout if I do."

Tatiana had never tried a mix before, but once she started, it was fun. She pretended she was in her own lab, the Tatiana Kumpf Scientific Discovery Unit. The measuring cups and bowls were beakers and flasks. Her apron was a lab coat. The oven was a special electromagnetic reactor.

At half-time, Dad came into the kitchen. He was heavy-set like Tatiana, with the same wide cheekbones and square jaw. His hair was thinning on top, and his face was creased – worried-looking much of the time, but with a wonderful crinkly smile when he was relaxed, at times like this.

"They look good," he said. "Any free samples?"

"The broken ones, and the ones over there that are overdone. But don't touch the others!"

"OK, boss." He tasted one. "Mmm. Any chance of a few for my lunch tomorrow?"

"The rejects are free," Tatiana said. "The others are five pence each." She filled another baking sheet.

It was late when Tatiana took the last biscuits out of the oven and packed them into labelled shoeboxes. Dad rarely noticed things like bedtimes. She went to her room just as Mum got home.

"It smells wonderful in here!" Mum called. "How did things go?"

"All right."

Tatiana flopped into bed. She closed her eyes and tried to sleep, but all she saw were little balls of biscuit dough being spooned out, one after another after another.

Chapter Three
No Turning Back

THE GREAT BISCUIT Sale had come and gone. Tatiana stood in the school hall and counted her money, writing the numbers carefully. She checked her arithmetic, then shoved the paper under her books.

"You might as well have this." Nicola was

in front of her, offering half a sandwich. "I noticed you didn't get any lunch."

They hadn't spoken for two days.

"Thanks." Tatiana fumbled for words. "I – are you still angry?"

"You are so stubborn, Tatiana."

"I would have let you help me. Honest. But – "

Nicola smiled. "I know. You're just you. I'm glad it's over. Now maybe we can talk about something else for a change."

Tatiana held out the unsold biscuits. "Have some." It was good to be friends again.

After school they headed home together.

"It's so much milder now," said Nicola softly. "On a cloudy day like this, everything's two colours. Have you noticed? The sky's white, and the snow's white, but the fences and trees and bushes are all brown. It's like those old photographs, you know?"

Tatiana nodded. "Sepia," she said.

"Winter's interesting, isn't it?" said Nicola. "It's always different."

Tatiana stood for a moment, thinking, staring in front of her.

"Come on, then," Nicola said.

They turned into Nicola's driveway, which led to a double garage and a ramp going to the side door. Tatiana followed Nicola in. The thick carpets, soft furniture, bright cushions, houseplants and big windows always gave her a feeling of warmth and comfort.

Nicola reached for the CD player, filling the room with soft music. "All right," she said, "how much money did you make?"

The warm feeling left. Tatiana took a deep

breath and spoke fast. "I sold one hundred and seventy-one biscuits," she said, "at five pence each." She pulled out her paper. "That's eight pounds fifty-five."

Nicola nodded.

"And I bought four packets of biscuit mix at one pound twenty-nine each."

"Biscuit mix?"

"That comes to five pounds sixteen. Which means that for all that work I made a profit of three pounds and thirty-nine pence."

Nicola was silent. She didn't say Tatiana should have charged more than five pence each. She didn't say recipes from scratch would have been cheaper. She looked at Tatiana. "That's too bad," she said. "You worked so hard on it."

"Well, that's the bad news." Tatiana stuffed

the paper back into her school bag. "Now the good news. I have a topic for my project."

"You have?"

"I thought of it coming home just now. You gave me the clue."

"I did?"

"'Winter's interesting', you said. And you're right."

"You're doing it on winter?"

"No, that's too general. But snow. Snow! Why is it white? Why do snowflakes have different patterns? How do they get that way? Think about it, Nicola, it's a great topic! Snow is everywhere at the moment, and it's free, and it was right under my nose all along!"

"There's certainly lots of it," Nicola said.

Later, Tatiana stood on a kitchen chair at

home, holding her arms straight out while Mum, bending and stretching, fitted and pinned. She frowned, trying to shift her mind to something more interesting. What would be the best way to narrow down her topic?

"Now hold still! How can I make this fit if you fidget all the time?"

"I'm not a statue, Mum! I feel like a scarecrow up here!"

"This dress will look lovely on you. It's a very slimming style."

"Jeans is all I need."

"I've noticed. That's why I'm making you something pretty."

Tatiana sighed. She was about to say something about looking pretty, but decided against it. "There's Dad!" The old blue Mini was out of sight now, but Tatiana had seen it turn in. A few minutes later she saw the top of Dad's head as he stopped to chat with Mrs McNair.

"I'd forgotten the time." Mum gathered the sewing things.

The front door banged.

"Hello, Peter." Mum turned towards him.

Dad walked right past her. "Tatiana!"

"Huh?" Tatiana was trying to pull the dress over her head without being pricked by pins.

"What exactly was this biscuit sale?"

Pins were still catching in her T-shirt and jeans. "It was at lunchtime today," Tatiana said. "I told you about it. You were right here when I was making them."

"Yes, and you told me it was for school fundraising."

"Yes."

"Then why did Mrs McNair just tell me that you raised the money for yourself?"

"It's for my Science Fair project." Tatiana scuffed her trainers on the floor. "I got permission from the science teacher. I needed the money for expenses."

Mum looked up from folding the dress. "You never said that's what it was for. I thought it was for charity."

"My daughter is not charity." Dad's face was red, and the veins bulged at the side of his forehead. "My daughter does not beg in the neighbourhood. Do you understand me?"

Tatiana nodded.

"If you need money, ask for it. All right?"

Tatiana nodded again.

"But Peter, she did ask for it." Mum twisted a tape measure absent-mindedly in one hand. "I told her she should save it up out of her allowance."

Dad took his wallet out of a back pocket. He was still wearing his overcoat, and a puddle grew from his shoes as the snow on them thawed. "How much do you need?"

Tatiana hesitated. "I'm not sure yet."

"How much did the sale make?"

"Three pounds and something."

"Is that all? What do you need, then? Five more? Ten? Speak up."

"Something like that." There would be film, and other equipment, thought Tatiana, though she hadn't had time to figure it all out. And it was hard to think with him looking through her like that.

Dad opened his wallet. He took out a five-pound note, then walked to the kitchen. Tatiana could see Mum watching the wet tracks he made. He took the food money from its place behind the cutlery drawer, and drew another five-pound note from it.

"There," he said, turning and slapping them into Tatiana's hands. "That's ten pounds. If you need more, say so. Now get busy with that project, all right? And be sure you see it through."

Tatiana nodded.

"By the way – Tatiana!"

She had started to her room, and turned back.

"Next time you try to sell, I'll show you how to make a profit. You should have more than three pounds something for all that work."

Tatiana nodded. "Thanks, Dad," she said.

"Peter," Mum said, "get your coat off and

help me peel potatoes, or we'll never have supper tonight. Tatiana, you set the table."

It was almost dark outside. Tatiana reached to close the kitchen curtains. It was snowing again lightly, and for a moment she stood there, watching the tiny white swirls in the dark blue sky.

There's no turning back now, she whispered to herself. I wanted to do this for myself, anyway. But now I'm going to do it for Dad, too.

Chapter Four
A Closer Look

THE NEXT MORNING the snow came in squalls of fat fluffy flakes. It was much colder.

Muffled in a thick coat, her hood pulled tightly around her face, and wearing mittens, two scarves, wool socks, and everything else

Mum had insisted on, Tatiana rushed outside.

She leaned over a snow-covered wall and peered through her stamp-collection magnifier.

"Tatty! What are you doing?"

William's voice. But where was he?

"Up here!"

Tatiana looked carefully at William's house next door. He was leaning out of an upstairs window, waving both arms to get her attention. Just as suddenly, he disappeared as if he'd been pulled backwards, and the window shut.

Tatiana sighed, and bent over again to look at the snow. For the millionth time she wished she had a different name. She hated people calling her Tatty. She hated having grown-ups say, "Tatiana! Isn't that a pretty name!" She hated being Tatiana Kumpf.

"Hello!" William was next to her. "My mum wasn't keen on me falling out of the window. I've been looking and looking, Tatty. Are you trying to start a campfire?"

"I am not Tatty," Tatiana grunted without looking up. "And I'm studying snow. For the Science Fair."

"Oh. Nicola said you were trying to think of a topic. We were having bets on how long you're gonna stick with it. I say a week, she says three, judging from the other times."

"What other times?" Tatiana straightened up.

"Well, there was the short-story contest. You had a good story, but –"

"But I couldn't get the ending right. That was different."

"I think you could do it," William said,

smiling. "You just have to put your mind to it. When Tatiana Alexandra Kumpf finally puts her mind to something, watch out, world!"

"How do you know my middle name?"

"I know a lot of things."

That was the trouble with William. He did know a lot of things.

"William!" Mrs McNair's voice, insistent.

"Uh-oh," said William. "My mum wants to take me shopping. She says my mittens don't match." He loped off in the direction of the voice. "I don't know why it matters. They're warm, just the same. See you, Tatty."

"Tatiana!" she shouted after him.

Tatiana held the magnifier over her sleeve and examined the snowflakes that drifted on to it. The crystals were mostly broken or piled on top of each other. But sometimes, against the dark fabric, she saw one that looked perfect — beautiful, fragile, perfect.

She stayed there for a long time, thinking it out, mumbling to herself. "That's what I'll do. I'll take photos of snowflakes. I'll *show* that no two snowflakes are exactly alike. That will impress the judges."

The wind picked up, and Tatiana headed inside. Her toes and fingers were almost numb, but she felt a new enthusiasm. The Science Fair was three weeks today. This would be her best project ever.

Inside, Mum was ladling soup. "We've just got time for a quick lunch before we visit Ida."

"Oh Mum! It's boring going to see old Ida." Mum and Ida used to do embroidery together. "Ida doesn't know me any more. She pats me on the head like

I'm a three-year-old."

"She likes seeing you."

It was true. And deep down, Tatiana didn't mind seeing the old lady. But not today. Today she wanted to buy film and take pictures of snowflakes. Suddenly she thought of something.

"Remember that magnifier you gave Ida once? That big one on a stand, so she'd have her hands free for sewing?"

"Yes."

"Would she let me borrow it?"

"I expect so. She probably can't use it any more."

They finished lunch, and hurried to the bus stop. William and his mother were coming home next door, and William was struggling with two lumpy, heavy-looking grocery bags.

"Hello, William," said Mum. "What have you got there?"

"That's all the woollies she made me buy," William said.

"William!" said Mrs McNair.

William grinned. "No, this winter hasn't been *that* cold. It's my cabbages."

Cabbages? thought Tatiana. It did look like cabbages. But what in the world did William McNair want cabbages for?

Tatiana did not see William again until school the following week, but she knew better than to ask him about his cabbages anyway. "You never know when he gives a straight answer, and when he's joking," she said to Nicola as they trudged home one day.

Tatiana had Dad's camera, and the film,

and Ida's magnifier. But by the time they'd come home from Ida's last week it was dark, and since then there had been no new snow. Not one flake.

"Things always go wrong and stop me doing things," Tatiana complained. "It's not my fault."

"Well, here's good news," said Nicola. "Amy said she'll help you look things up on Saturday. With the computer, you know?"

"I don't want to bother Amy."

"Tatiana, she offered. Let her help you. I'll be there too."

But on Saturday, it was Amy who answered the door at the Jensons' house.

"Hello," she said, swinging her wheelchair back towards the family room. "Nicola had an extra ballet practice. That show they're doing. You're in perfect time."

Tatiana pulled out her notebook.

One thing she had not counted on was spending the morning with just Amy. She hardly knew Amy. She never knew what to say when Amy was around. "Nicola's good at ballet, isn't she?" she muttered.

"Yeah." Amy turned on the computer. "She was always more graceful at it than I was."

"You did ballet?"

"Of course," Amy smiled. "We used to do duets. Like I say, she was more graceful. I was stronger than her, but she was more graceful."

Tatiana had never known Amy except in her wheelchair. She couldn't imagine her walking, let alone doing things like ballet. What sort of sickness did Amy have? She had never thought of that before.

Amy was busy hitting keys and watching the screen.

"What are you doing there?" Tatiana asked, partly to change the subject.

"Just signing on. It'll connect in a second, and then we can access the database." Amy paused, and looked at the screen. "Right. Now, what do you want to search for?"

"Snow," said Tatiana.

"Snow? OK, but you'd better be more specific, or we'll have two tons of material."

They leaned forward, staring at the screen, figuring out subject headings.

Inuit words for snow. The shape of snowflakes. Snowflake Bentley, pioneer researcher. There was so much information there.

Amy typed some more, then sat back.

"I've got the log open," she said, "so it's

saving to disk. We'll print it up after."

Masses of text rushed up the screen at blurry-eyed speed.

"There," said Amy, "I signed off. That won't cost much. Isn't it neat?"

Tatiana nodded. "Fantastic."

"I'll print it up." Amy sneezed. "As soon as I blow my nose again. I think I'm getting a cold."

"I guess you have to be careful," said Tatiana, "with germs and stuff."

"No more careful than anyone else." Amy loaded paper into the printer.

Briefly, just briefly, Tatiana had felt comfortable with Amy. Now she felt awkward again.

"Well, I just thought –".

"You thought I'd get sick and die if I catch a cold? Is that what you thought?"

"No, Amy, I –"

"Listen." Amy's round face was serious. "Just because I'm in a wheelchair doesn't mean I'm sick, OK? Didn't Nicola ever tell you?"

Tatiana shook her head.

Amy's voice was even, matter-of-fact. "There was a place we used to swim in the country," she said. "The first time we went swimming that year, Nicola said the water was too cold. I said she was chicken, and I just dived in."

Her voice softened, barely audible above the rattle of the printer. "How was I supposed to know there was a log there, that wasn't there the year before?"

Chapter Five
That William!

"Oh, Amy!"

"Don't feel sorry for me." Amy leaned over the printer. "It was a stupid thing to do, that's all. And I can do anything I put my mind to, whether I'm in a wheelchair or not."

"Of course you can."

All the way home Tatiana thought about Amy. She tried to imagine her, tough, athletic, exuberant, out-running, out-jumping, out-diving everyone.

She felt sorry for Amy, yet a nagging thought pestered her. She, Tatiana, would have checked the water first. She was always methodical like that, even if people teased her about it.

She looked down at the papers clutched in her mittened hands. Two weeks today was the Science Fair. It was OK to be methodical.

When Tatiana got home, Mum and Dad were reading the paper over cold cups of coffee. Dad always took things easy on his Saturdays off.

"You just missed William," Mum said.

"What did he want?"

"He said you can borrow his dad's tripod."

"I never asked for a tripod."

Dad lowered his paper. "You'll need one if you're going to take pictures of snowflakes. It holds the camera still."

"How did William know I was taking pictures?"

"I suppose someone told him." Dad chuckled. "That boy William."

"What?"

"He wanted cabbage recipes," said Mum. "So I gave him my cabbage-roll recipe. But your father –"

Dad shook his head. "I gave him that old sauerkraut recipe from my German grandmother. Can you imagine the McNairs with a crock of that in their house? It doesn't just smell, it stinks!"

"But William was delighted with it," giggled Mum. "What's going on? Is he taking up cooking or something?"

"I have no idea," Tatiana said. "William is silly. He's always doing things to get attention."

By mid-afternoon, when Nicola dropped by, Tatiana was in her room drawing snowflake patterns on a large piece of poster board.

"I hear you and Amy got good stuff," Nicola said.

"Mmm." Tatiana's chin was almost on the paper, and her tongue showed at one side of her mouth as she frowned in concentration. "I've almost finished this one," she said. "See? Some snowflake patterns are hexagons, like this, and some are the feathery, Christmassy kind. But no two are ever the same."

Nicola nodded. She moved the rock collection off Tatiana's bed and sat watching. "It looks good," she said. After a while she stretched. "I brought some doughnuts. All that ballet made me hungry."

Tatiana got up slowly, looking at the final poster critically with her head on one side. "I think I'm getting somewhere at last," she said. "For the first time, I've got it all sorted out in my mind. The main part will be my photos, showing how the crystals are all different. But I'll have posters, too. I'll tell about weather – meteorology – what snow is, and such. Do you know why snow's white?"

"No," said Nicola, handing out doughnuts, "but I'm glad it is."

"It's because of the light, reflecting off all those tiny snow crystals. There was this farmer in Vermont, Snowflake Bentley. He took thousands of photographs of snow crystals using a microscope, and each one was different."

"You've got a good topic," Nicola said, licking jam off her fingers.

"They've all got six sides, because of the way the water molecules stick together. You see —" Tatiana stopped. There was a blank expression on Nicola's face. "Well, anyway, it's coming together. How was your ballet?"

"Fine." Nicola seemed pleased to change the subject. "I hope you like it on Friday. It was nice of your mum to get tickets."

Tatiana said nothing. Mum never stopped talking about Nicola and her ballet, and how slim and pretty and graceful Nicola was.

"I'll give them to her now, before I go." Nicola fished in her pockets. "And I have to deliver this to William, too." She pulled out a recipe card.

"Is that another cabbage recipe?"

"Yes, cabbage salad."

"Nicola, why is William going berserk over cabbage recipes?"

Nicola smiled. "For his project."

"What project?"

"Didn't he tell you?" Nicola's smile faded. "Oh, I thought you knew. William's decided to enter the Science Fair."

Tatiana stood staring. "William? Why didn't you tell me?"

"I thought you knew. Everyone at school knows. You were there when he was asking Mr P about the botanical names for cabbage?"

"I don't remember that." But Tatiana did remember him asking something, and the class laughing. She tended to tune out when William had attention.

"I'm sorry," Nicola said. "You told me about the bags of cabbages, and I thought you knew."

"But – he's doing it on cabbages?"

Nicola shrugged. "Something like that."

Tatiana crumpled the doughnut bag and absent-mindedly threw out the rest of her doughnut with it. "Well, that's the end of me. No way can I win if William's going in for it."

"Of course you can! You've got a great project." They headed into the kitchen. "Here's the tickets, Mrs Kumpf."

"Thank you." Mum rummaged in her purse. "I haven't seen ballet for ages. Did I tell you I once danced in a television commercial?"

"Mother!" said Tatiana.

After Nicola left, Tatiana flopped on her bed. Her project was awful. Snow was a stupid topic. How could she prove that all snowflakes are different? Even if she took a million photographs, she couldn't prove that.

William didn't care about being a scientist. He wanted to be an artist or a comedian or an engineer, depending on which day you asked. William could be anything he wanted to be. It wasn't fair.

"Everyone I know is good at something," Tatiana muttered. "Nicola's good at ballet. Amy's good at maths and computers." She punched at her pillow. "And William's good at everything."

She slouched into the living room.

"William's entering the Science Fair."

"That's nice." Mum did not look up.

"Nicola says he's doing it on cabbages."

"Really."

Tatiana sighed. Dad did not seem to have heard at all.

Nicola's recipe card was on the kitchen table.

"I'm going next door for a minute," Tatiana said.

In some ways, William was the last person she wanted to see. But she needed to check things out.

And today, at the McNairs' house, there was an unmistakable odour of cabbage.

"Hello, Tatty. Thanks!" William seemed pleased. "I'll get the tripod."

"It doesn't matter," Tatiana said.

William's blue eyes widened. "You haven't

quit, have you?"

"I didn't say that." Her face felt flushed. "Well, I suppose I'll take it, while I'm here."

Tatiana followed William upstairs. His house was cluttered and comfortable, with books and thick glossy magazines everywhere. It was an old house compared to Nicola's, but it still had everything: CD player, colour TV, video, dishwasher, computer. At Tatiana's there were three radios and one second-hand TV, and the dishwashers were all two-legged.

William pulled the tripod out of a cupboard. "So, how's your project going?"

"OK. I didn't know you were entering."

William laughed. "Yeah, just for fun. Want to see what I've got so far?"

Tatiana nodded. Her heart was pounding.

He opened the door to a spare room.

Tatiana gasped. Pots of seedlings sat on the windowsill, next to a half-empty bag of potting soil. Unfinished charts and notes and drawings covered every available space, along with cabbages, erasers, crayons, spoons, marker pens, books and junk. A waste-paper basket sat on a shelf, empty.

"It's a bit of a mess," William admitted. "But you seemed to be enjoying your project, and I thought, what the heck. It'll be something to do."

"You're doing it on cabbages?"

William's eyes twinkled. "Listen, those judges will see all kinds of serious projects. Things like yours, Tatty, that are aiming to win. So I figured I'd give them something to cheer them up. Make them laugh."

"But what about the recipes?"

"Ah, that's my challenge. Cabbage is

nutritious, see. It's got vitamin C, for one thing. So I'm making up menus for a whole day's food – and everything'll have cabbage in it."

Tatiana grimaced.

"Cabbage juice isn't so bad," he said. "But I tried a cabbage cake using my mum's carrot cake recipe, and it didn't come out so good. Hey – look at this!"

William picked up a large cabbage.

"Oh, William!" she said.

He had carved out the inside and part of the rest of the cabbage, and proudly held the biggest – well, the only – cabbage jack-o'-lantern that Tatiana had ever seen.

Chapter Six
Cold Comfort

BY FRIDAY IT was raining, sheeting against the windows out of a dull grey sky. Snow melted in sloppy puddles. Water gurgled down gutters and drainpipes.

The Science Fair was one week tomorrow.

Mum darted gracefully around the

kitchen, making supper. "It looks like that cold snap is over at last," she said.

"I hope not," said Tatiana. "I need snow for my photographs."

"Tatiana, don't be so hard on yourself. You made nice drawings. You don't have to have photos, too."

"That's the important part," Tatiana said. "You have to have a problem, or a purpose. I wanted to prove that all snowflakes are different."

"I don't know how you'd do that, with just a few pictures. And you did leave it rather late."

Tatiana sighed. "It's not *my* fault it stopped snowing."

Mum handed her place mats. "Now hurry and set the table. Tonight's Nicola's ballet, remember?"

She remembered. Mum had talked of little else all week.

That evening in a crowded church hall, wedged between Mum and Mrs Jenson, Tatiana yawned as she watched groups of dancers come and go. She was only interested in seeing Nicola. To her right, beyond Mrs Jenson, Amy sat in her wheelchair in the aisle.

At last the senior girls danced on. "Where's Nicola?" Tatiana whispered.

"Sshh!" Mum said.

The girls danced the first part of their piece, then the spotlight followed another dancer on to the stage. Tatiana sat transfixed. It was Nicola. Her hair was swept up and she wore the most beautiful filmy tutu. When Nicola danced she was part of the music, transformed by it. She hardly seemed to touch the floor.

"Wow!" Tatiana breathed in spite of herself.

She glanced at Mum. Mum was nodding her head in time to the music, with an expression of joy that Tatiana had rarely seen before.

Almost, just for a moment, Tatiana wished that she was graceful and slim and feminine like Nicola – like Mum. Maybe then she would have done ballet, and she wouldn't be worrying about Science Fairs and snowflake photos.

Tatiana tugged at the dress Mum had made her wear. It was tight and uncomfortable.

The music ended. There was a hush, then applause.

"Well done, Nicola!" Amy's voice.

Nicola curtsied in front of the footlights,

and smiled at her sister.

The programme continued, but for Tatiana it was over. She looked along the row, fidgeting. Amy was not watching the stage either. She was slouched in her wheelchair, looking wilted and sad.

Afterwards, the crowd spilled into the small foyer. "She was just wonderful," Mum gushed to Mrs Jenson.

Tatiana headed outside with Amy. It had stopped raining now, and felt colder.

"The weather forecast said it might snow tonight," Amy said, "but I hope not. It's hard enough getting around in this stupid wheelchair."

There was a rare bitterness in Amy's voice. She shoved ahead past Tatiana through the crowd, towards the Jenson van.

Walking home next to Mum, Tatiana

thought about Nicola, and Amy. She tried not to think about Amy's dreadful sadness.

In the middle of the night Tatiana woke to hear heavy rain hammering down. The forecast must have been wrong. She jammed her pillow around her head, muffling her ears from the sound. It wasn't fair.

The next morning, Saturday, Tatiana slept in. There was nothing to get up for. It was quiet outside; the rain must have stopped at last. She vaguely heard her parents in the kitchen, and the door downstairs closing as Dad left for work.

When she did get up and open her bedroom curtains, Tatiana stood for a moment, not believing. Then she raced out of her room.

"Mum! Mum! Why didn't you tell me?"

A note lay on the table: "I'm downstairs

doing the washing. Back in a minute. Mum."

Snowflakes! Tatiana ran to each window in turn. Thousands – millions – of them, drifting down. Big, fluffy, white, beautiful, snowflakes!

She rushed to the telephone and dialled with fumbling fingers. "Nicola? Listen, I slept in. Have you seen the snow? Isn't it perfect? Can you come over? OK, see you soon!"

Tatiana gathered everything together. She peered through the balcony glass to check the thermometer outside. She tapped Dad's little barometer. She wrote all the numbers down.

Where was Nicola? She checked the thermometer again. The temperature was dropping.

She snapped on the radio. Snow was

forecast all day, with a biting easterly wind expected to drop the temperature to minus five degrees Celsius by lunchtime. Minus five degrees. Tatiana thought for a moment. Wow!

By the time Nicola arrived, she was almost dancing with excitement.

"Leave your things on," she said, "and follow me. I've got a great idea."

"Tatiana," Nicola said, "do you know you're still wearing pyjamas?"

"I am?" Tatiana looked down. "Oh, you're right. Well, no one will notice."

She pulled on her duffle coat, scarf, hat, socks and boots, and led the way through the living room, sliding open the glass door to the apartment balcony. They set up a card table there, nearest the outer edge.

"I've got a new angle," Tatiana said. "I

can't *prove* that snowflakes are all different, but maybe I can prove what happens to them when it gets colder."

"What does happen?"

"They get smaller." Tatiana held up her notebook. "My theory – I just figured this out – is that ice crystals stick together more when it's milder, so the snowflakes *look* big and fluffy. And when it's colder they're more separate, so the snowflakes look small."

Nicola smiled. "And you've got a thermometer right here," she said.

"Right." Tatiana lifted a piece of black card towards the gently swirling snow. She waited for it to be covered with snowflakes.

"Did you like my ballet?" Nicola asked.

"Yes, it was nice." Tatiana set the paper quickly on the table. Under Ida's magnifier, each snowflake was clearly a group of separate ice crystals piled on top of each other. The crystals were transparent, with a six-sided shape that was often broken or partially melted. But a few were perfect.

"I was nervous," said Nicola. "My knees were shaking when I was waiting to go on. But once you start dancing, it's different."

"Fantastic!" Tatiana said. She shook the paper, and gathered more snowflakes. "Take a look, but be careful. They melt if you breathe on them."

Nicola sighed. "Well, your mum liked it, anyway."

She bent over the magnifier. "Wow! Oh, they do melt when you breathe on them."

"It's coming up to minus one degree Celsius. Bring over that tripod, OK? I screwed the camera on to it and set it up like Dad said."

They soon got into a rhythm. Nicola collected snowflakes on a fresh piece of black card. Tatiana put it under the magnifier, took the picture, shook the snowflakes off and reached out her hand for the next paper. They didn't talk much, and they worked fast.

After seven pictures Tatiana leaned back, dug her hands into her pockets and waited.

"Is that it?" asked Nicola. She was shivering, and her cheeks were red.

"Of course not," replied Tatiana. "We have to wait for the temperature to drop another degree. Then we'll take the next batch. They said on the radio that it's going down to minus five, so I can get five groups of snowflake pictures at different temperatures. And with seven pictures each time, that'll be thirty-five pictures out of my roll of thirty-six."

"Oh," Nicola said.

"One of the things the judges are looking for is 'Adequate data to support conclusion', see?" Tatiana had never felt so confident. "This one's a winner, Nicola."

Nicola pulled her hood farther forward and tied the strings.

They had finished the third batch of pictures, at minus three degrees Celsius, when Mum banged on the glass from inside.

"Don't open it!" shouted Tatiana. "I don't want warm air out here."

"I can hardly feel my fingers," Nicola said.

"Won't be long. The temperature's dropping fast. We're almost at minus four."

Soon Mum banged on the glass again. This time she slid the door open as well.

"You girls come in now," she said. "You'll get frostbite."

"I think I will, Mrs Kumpf. I'm really cold." Nicola stepped inside. "Come in and warm up a bit, Tatiana."

"No way," Tatiana said. "Shut the door, shut the door. I'm staying till this is finished."

Chapter Seven
It's Not Fair!

FOR ONCE MUM didn't argue. Tatiana took the next photos by herself, then peeked through the glass inside. Mum and Nicola were drinking something hot, and Nicola had a blanket wrapped around her.

Tatiana shivered. She waited and waited,

checking the thermometer. Just one more little degree to go. It seemed stuck at minus four Celsius. For the first time, she wished she had on something warmer than pyjamas under her coat.

Her toes felt numb, and she almost shook with cold. But the results will be worth it, she told herself. I'm not quitting this time. She blew into her stiff fingers to warm them.

At last! Minus five degrees! Tatiana took the last seven pictures.

Heat from the living room flooded over her as she trundled back inside.

"I did it! I did it!" Her face was so cold, it almost hurt to speak.

"Good for you," said Mum. "Have some cocoa. Nicola and I were just talking about the ballet."

Tatiana began to take off her coat, remembered the pyjamas, and sidled to her room. She dressed, then carefully removed the film from the camera.

Nicola was about to leave.

"I'll go with you to the town centre," Tatiana said, gulping down her drink. "They do one-hour photos. When I come back, I'll have breakfast, Mum."

"Breakfast!" Mum's voice followed them downstairs. "It's almost lunchtime!"

They sat on a bench near the camera shop while they waited.

"Last week I almost quit," Tatiana said.

"I thought you had quit," said Nicola, "until you phoned this morning. William thought you'd quit, too."

"Well, I didn't." She paused. "And I'm not

going to. I've figured it all out, and I can hardly wait to see how they –"

"Are my pictures ready yet?" The voice at the counter sounded familiar. William turned, and saw them. "Oh hello! Want to see my pictures for the Science Fair?"

Tatiana's stomach tightened. "All right."

He opened the envelope. "They came out better than I thought," he chuckled, passing along the pictures one by one.

They were taken in the grocery department, with staff in increasingly silly poses holding up broccoli, Brussels sprouts, cauliflower and several different kinds of cabbage.

Nicola giggled. Tatiana smiled in spite of herself.

"I wanted to show all the cabbage relatives as well," William said. "A lot of veggies come from the brassica family."

Tatiana felt tired and hungry. "I'll get mine," she said.

When she returned, they had photos spread all over the bench.

"They used to think cabbages could cure plagues and remove freckles," William said. "Think of that, Tatty. Some of my good cabbage juice and your freckles will be gone forever."

"I don't have freckles," said Tatiana. "And my name, for the millionth time, is Tatiana. How would you like it if I called you Billy all the time? I'm Tatiana, OK?"

"OK," William said.

"And I don't have freckles. Get that through your thick skull, all right?"

William shrugged. "All right."

"How did yours come out, Tatiana?" Nicola asked.

"I don't know. I haven't opened them yet."

William gathered up his photos. "I gotta go," he said. "Bye, Tat-i-ana."

Tatiana glared after him. "That William makes me so mad."

"You didn't have to be mean to him."

"I wasn't. I'm just tired of his silliness."

"He's funny. And he means well. You're just jealous because his pictures turned out so good."

"Jealous? Is that what you think?"

"Tatiana." Nicola leaned forward. "Your pictures will be good, too. Why don't you open them?"

"I will," said Tatiana. "When I get home. I'm starving."

"You're just scared to look. I know you."

It wasn't until Tatiana was inside her block of flats that she finally stopped, took a deep breath, and ripped open the envelope. She peeked quickly at the snowflake pictures, sighed, and headed up the stairs.

Mum was busy with material and pins.

"You're not sewing me another dress," Tatiana said.

"No, this one's for me. I wanted something new for a change." She smoothed pattern pieces with her hands. "I have a feeling I'm going to need it."

"What for?" Tatiana sat down and studied her pictures.

"For the awards ceremony. Didn't you say parents are invited?"

Tatiana looked up. "What awards ceremony?"

"For the Science Fair."

"But I won't win, Mum!"

"That's what you're aiming for, isn't it?

You're closer than you've ever been. I never saw you work so hard. I don't have much time for sewing, and –"

"Mum –"

"I was thinking about it after Nicola's ballet." She reached for scissors and started to cut. "You're not like Nicola, not at all. But you shine at other things, once you put your mind to it. I just want to be ready."

"Mum, I'll be in it. But I'm not going to win. I can't win against William. Look at this." She threw the photos on to the coffee table.

Mum picked them up. "They're nice. Very nice."

"Look at them. Some of them are blurry. Or they're too dark. Or the ice crystals melted. There isn't one *perfect* picture in the whole roll."

"Perfect? Who says you have to be perfect? They're all right, Tatiana. Snowflakes are difficult to photograph."

"Mum, sew yourself something nice. But don't count on wearing it for me, OK? William's got the funniest, cleverest photos for his project and they all came out perfect. Nothing I do ever comes out right."

Tatiana felt tired all over, and her throat was sore. The energy seemed to have drained out of her.

Later, helping Dad with the washing up, she still felt miserable. If I was smart and clever and creative like William, she told herself, I could make the judges laugh, too.

"Dad, can you think of a way to make snowflakes funny?"

"Funny?" Dad's eyes widened. "No," he said. "Snowflakes are not funny. Cold. Heavy to sweep away. Pretty sometimes. But not funny."

Tatiana sighed. "The only good thing is, they *are* smaller in colder weather. I can see that. And I think I can measure it. But I want the judges to notice."

"Oh, they'll notice. That's their job. Are you working on it this evening?"

"No." She tried to avoid his look. "I don't feel like it."

For days Tatiana did not feel like it. There was only the final write-up to do, and the graphs. That wouldn't take long.

By the end of school on Thursday, Tatiana had a bad cold and cough. Amy wheeled beside her.

"Tatiana," she said, "are there ramps at the arena?"

"I think so. Why?"

"I hate being carried places. I'm going to the Science Fair on Saturday, with Nicola. I want to see you beat William."

"I don't know about that."

"I want to see you beat him. You can do it. It'll be good for him to be beaten for a change." She looked at Tatiana sharply. "You are still going in it, aren't you? You haven't quit again?"

"I haven't quit. I'm doing the final write-up." It was hard to fool Amy.

Later that evening, Tatiana reached for her project. She set Dad's typewriter on the kitchen table. Mum was out at choir.

The first section was fun. She enjoyed explaining things like a real scientist: Introduction, Materials and Methods, Results and Discussion, Conclusion. But she wished she'd learned to type properly.

She stopped to blow her nose. Again. Two more days to the Science Fair. Even methodical people need a deadline sometimes.

She was part way into the second section, on snowflake research, when the typewriter carriage jammed. She pulled at the return lever. It moved easily – too easily.

"Dad!"

"Hhhh?" He was watching another football match.

"The typewriter's broken."

Dad looked at it, poked it, turned it upside down, shook it. The carriage return lever hung there, limp.

"That's never happened before," he said. He shook his head. "I can take it in for you tomorrow, but repairs take a while. There's nothing I can do. I'm sorry."

Chapter Eight
Countdown

"I WON'T LET anything stop me." Tatiana's hands were tight fists in her lap. "I'll think of something."

There was only one thing she could think of. She hated having to do it. She went to the telephone.

Nicola listened, as always. She said yes right away. "If you can dictate it, I'll type it tomorrow evening on our computer," she said.

The next day was Friday the thirteenth, but that didn't bother Tatiana.

"Good luck in the Science Fair," William said.

"Yeah," said Tatiana. "See you there." She paused. "Good luck, William."

After supper it was clear and cold as Tatiana hurried to Nicola's. She couldn't stop coughing, despite Mum's cough medicine, and her chest hurt.

"My dad said we could use his computer," Nicola said. "I haven't used it often, but I know how. I just have to be careful."

Tatiana spread out her papers. "I finished everything else last night," she said, "and

I left spaces for the parts that weren't typed. OK, new paragraph: Wilson Bentley took many photographs of ice crystals . . ."

Nicola was a good typist, but slow. The sky outside darkened from dusky blue to deep blue, navy and black. Tatiana coughed again, and shivered. She felt strange, somehow. She was glad Nicola was doing the typing.

"Tatiana!"

"What?"

"You had your eyes shut."

"Oh. I was just thinking."

By the time they got to the final section, the waste-paper basket was full of the crumpled notes Tatiana discarded as they finished each page.

"Not much more to go," she said, reaching

to turn on another light. "New sentence: There are a trillion water molecules in each snowflake."

"Think of that."

"High in a cloud, the molecules stick together in a hexagonal pattern –"

"How do you spell 'hexagonal'?" Nicola turned, and as she did, something at the window caught her attention. "Oh! Look at the moon!"

Tatiana looked, keeping one finger on her place.

"It's so beautiful," said Nicola. "All shimmery and magical and dreamy-looking. Just like on my poster, isn't it?"

"Mmm. Where were we?" Tatiana ached all over. She rested her head against the chair back.

But Nicola was lost for the moment,

staring out at the night sky. "'*Slowly, silently, now the moon, Walks the night in her silver shoon*'," she whispered. "That's by Walter de la Mare." She turned back to the computer, her face dreamy.

"Did you finish the bit about hexagonal?"

Nicola nodded. "I wrote a poem about the moon once," she said, yawning. "But it wasn't as good as that." Her hands moved over the keyboard again.

Suddenly Nicola stopped typing. She looked at the monitor, pressed some keys, then looked again.

"What is it?"

"I – I don't know. It won't type. The keys work, but – nothing happens."

Tatiana sat up and stared at the screen. Nicola was right. Whatever she did, nothing happened.

"The cursor's frozen," Nicola said. "I don't know why."

"Well, save it then."

Nicola shook her head. "I can't save it. I can't do anything. It's locked up on me."

"You're not telling me we've lost everything?"

Nicola spoke quietly. "I saved it as we went along," she said, "but I can't get at it. I don't know what I did. But I did something."

Tatiana stared at Nicola. Then her anger exploded. "So we just wasted this whole evening for nothing!" She pounded her notes into a ball and hurled them in the waste-paper basket. "Thanks a lot. First there's no snow, then the stupid typewriter breaks down, and now this. There's no way I can finish now before tomorrow."

"You don't have to yell at me." Nicola reached for the computer manual. "Just give me a minute, OK?"

"I don't have a minute. I need that stuff now!"

Nicola's face was flushed. "Listen," she said, banging the manual down on the desk. "I didn't mean it, OK? I did the best I could for you. And it wasn't me that left it to the last minute. I'm sick of hearing about you and your stupid project."

"You are the stupidest, dreamiest person I ever met!" shouted Tatiana.

"And you are the stubbornest, meanest person I ever met!" yelled back Nicola. "I don't know why I ever picked you for a friend."

"Well I wish you hadn't! So there! And I'm going home!"

"Good!" Nicola said. "The sooner you go the better, *Tatty* Kumpf!"

Amy rushed in. "What's going on in here?"

Tatiana felt hot and cold and shivery. Her chest hurt from the shouting. "I'm leaving," she said, "that's what's going on."

"It froze up on me," Nicola said. "Look!" She started to cry.

"Oh, Nicola!" said Amy.

Tatiana pushed past them, coughing, into the front hall.

Amy followed. "Hold on," she said, "there may be some way to fix it. That happens sometimes, you know?"

"I don't have time," said Tatiana. "I've already wasted enough time on you two." She pulled on her coat and jammed her feet into her boots. Her mittens hung out of her pockets, and her scarf was stuck in one sleeve.

Amy shoved her wheelchair in Tatiana's path. "Do you know that Nicola didn't have supper tonight on account of you leaving things to the last minute? By the time she got home from ballet there wasn't time. If it wasn't for Nicola, you wouldn't have got this far."

"Let me go." Tatiana pushed at Amy's wheelchair.

Nicola tossed her hair away from her tear-stained face. "Let her go," she said, her voice flat. "See if I care."

Tatiana stuck out her tongue at each of them. She charged outside, slammed the Jenson front door behind her, and stomped off in a fury towards home.

It was bitterly cold now, with patches of

ice on the road, but Tatiana hardly noticed. That Nicola. She shouldn't have offered if she didn't know how to use the thing. She was hopeless. Absolutely hopeless.

"The main thing," Tatiana shouted into the wind, "is to do things on your own. Forget other people. I should have done it all on my own and not said one word to anyone."

It was hard to see clearly. Sometimes things seemed to blur in front of her. She leaned against a post, then yanked up her hood as the wind and cold stung with its full force. Nicola's words stung just as bitterly.

"She called me Tatty," Tatiana stormed. "She called me stubborn and mean. She said she didn't know why she picked me for a friend. Well, now I know. She's been pretending to be my friend all along, but what she really wanted was to be Mum's friend. 'Oh, Nicola, isn't ballet wonderful! What a graceful, beautiful girl Nicola is!' "

And that Amy. Just because Amy was in a wheelchair didn't mean she could boss everyone around.

Tatiana plunged her hands more deeply into her pockets, ignoring the mittens. Her teeth chattered and her chest hurt — a lot — every time she coughed.

"I was so close, too. If that was my computer I'd know how to use it."

Her nose and cheeks hurt from the cold. It seemed a long way home. "It's not fair!" she mumbled. "Every time I try things, something stops me. That kite contest, the short-story contest, now this. I can't ever finish things. Now everyone will say I'm a quitter again." She pulled her hood farther forward.

Halfway across the road, Tatiana stopped for an instant, jerked back to reality. A car was coming towards her. Even with her hood up, she could see the lights as it came round the curve.

"Hey!" she shouted, and turned back.

The road was shiny and slippery. Everything looked strange. Tatiana's feet slid from under her. She tried to get up, staggering to regain her balance.

The lights were still coming at her.

Chapter Nine
All in Pieces

"TATIANA!" THE VOICE came from far away, insistent. "Can you open your eyes for me?"

Tatiana opened her eyes. A nurse with curly yellow hair was leaning close, smiling.

"How are you feeling?"

"Sleepy." Tatiana's voice was high, soft. She couldn't get it to come out any louder.

"I'm taking your temperature and pulse. You had quite a fever last night, young lady."

After a while the nurse patted her cheek. "Good," she said. "Now you rest. Your parents will be here again soon." She disappeared through the brown curtains that Tatiana now saw were around her bed.

Mum and Dad will be here again? When were they here before? Tatiana remembered cold, and voices, and being in someone's car. She wanted to sort it out, but her mind was fuzzy. What was she trying to sort out? She closed her eyes again, and slept.

"Hello, darling!" Mum and Dad were there.

"Hello." Tatiana focused her eyes. It was good to see them.

"You're awake at last," Dad said.

"I'm sleepy."

"That's because they gave you something. You needed it." Mum filled a glass with water and held it while Tatiana took sips.

She shut her eyes, then opened them. "Why am I here?"

"Don't you remember?"

Tatiana frowned. Pieces of a picture were in her mind. She tried to sit up, and a sharp pain stabbed. "Did I get hit by a car?"

"Well, bumped. The driver tried to stop, but he skidded on the ice. He felt terrible." Dad's worry lines showed, despite his smile. "It's just scrapes and bangs and bruises, thank God, though it took them a while to patch you up last night."

Mum stroked her forehead. "And once they got you in here they found out you have viral pneumonia! You must have felt awful, Tatiana. Why didn't you tell us you were so ill?"

"I didn't know I was." Tatiana tried to fit pieces together. "What day is today?"

"Saturday."

Saturday. What was it about Saturday that was important? The pain throbbed all over now, even when she wasn't moving.

By evening, Tatiana's mind began to clear, and she remembered the accident vividly. Bit by bit she also recalled what happened before it – the computer, and Nicola. And the Science Fair.

Why had Mum and Dad not said one word about it? And why did things always happen to her?

A woman pushed a trolley of flowers and gifts into the room. "T Kumpf – is that you?"

Tatiana nodded.

The woman handed her a card. Inside was a piece of paper with a poem on it, written in William's messy writing:

> Tatiana the brave, Tatiana the clever
> I'm sorry that you would ever ever
> Get hit by a car – winter is silly
> Get well soon,
> From your friend,
> Billy.
> AKA William Alexander McNair
> (PS now you know why I remembered your middle name is Alexandra).

Tatiana smiled. He'd called her Tatiana.

Just before bed, a nurse picked up another envelope from the night table. "Did you see this? It isn't opened."

"No." Tatiana looked at the fat envelope and her stomach went tight. She would know that flowing writing anywhere. Nicola.

It would be a long letter, probably listing all the reasons Nicola would never ever be her friend again.

An image of Nicola with her pale, angry, tear-stained face stuck in Tatiana's head. Tatiana had never seen her so angry.

The nurse tucked her in, and left. Tatiana pulled the cord that turned out the light above her bed. In the semi-darkness, she held Nicola's envelope tightly in her hand.

Everything had been going well until Nicola lost her temper. No, thought Tatiana soberly, I was the one who got angry first. I was mean. Nicola hadn't even had supper. And now I've lost the best friend anyone could ever have.

Suddenly she tore the envelope and its contents unopened into tiny pieces, dropping them one by one into the rubbish bag next to her bed. Then, softly, muffled by the pillow, she cried.

Mum and Dad visited again in the morning. But they changed the subject when she mentioned the Science Fair. "Don't you worry about anything," Dad said. "You'll be home today or tomorrow."

What was going on in the world? After they left, Tatiana looked for the pieces of Nicola's letter in the rubbish bag. Only an old magazine was in there. The bag had already been emptied.

"Hello!" Nicola was standing in the doorway.

"Oh!"

They looked at each other. Neither moved.

"Well, can I come in?"

"Of course." Tatiana grabbed the magazine, as if that was what she'd been looking for.

Nicola perched stiffly on the edge of a chair. Her face was serious.

"I – didn't expect you to come," Tatiana mumbled.

"I almost didn't, but Sunday's the only day kids can visit. Did you get my note?"

Tatiana nodded. Her heart was pounding.

"I was really cross with you."

"I know."

"I never felt so angry in my whole life."

Nicola looked towards the window, her voice a whisper. "If only you thought of other people's feelings more, you know?"

Tatiana stared at the floor. If she'd known Nicola was coming, she could have thought what to say. "I didn't know you hadn't eaten," she blurted out.

"Well, there was no way you would have waited. I know you." Nicola sighed. She looked at Tatiana. "I'm sorry I made that mistake, though. And like I said in the note, I felt awful about your accident."

Tatiana felt all churned up inside. Nicola was silent.

"Nicola —" Tatiana hesitated. "I — I shouldn't have blown up like that. I — you helped me, and I never thanked you."

Nicola looked at Tatiana. She seemed to be waiting for something.

Is she expecting me to ask about the Science Fair? Or was that in the note?

"You could say you're sorry," Nicola said.

"Oh!" said Tatiana. "Oh, yes. I am sorry, Nicola." It felt good to say it. "And I didn't mean all those things I said."

Nicola let out a big breath, and leaned back against her chair. "And I didn't mean what I said, either." She smiled. "Well, most of it. Hey, how did you feel when you read my note?"

"Oh, that was quite a note." Tatiana swallowed hard.

Nicola's face was dreamy. "It's funny, but it was thinking of my ballet that did it. You know how I want to go for an audition at the National Ballet School some day?"

"Yes."

"Well, I want that more than anything in

the whole world. So it's worth all the pain and the practising and the sore muscles, you know? If you want something important, so it hurts, you really have to go for it. Just like you and the Science Fair."

Tatiana nodded and looked away, wondering how to change the subject. Was this what had been in the note?

"Well, I thought how I'd feel if I got that close to an audition, and something happened."

There was a sudden commotion in the hall, and William and Amy burst in.

Chapter Ten
Watch Out, World!

AMY WAS JUST in front. "Beat you!" she said.

"Not fair," said William, breathless. "People got out of your way." He flopped on a chair. "Hey, Tatty! How are you doing? Did you get my card?"

"Yes, William. Thanks. And I liked the poem."

"So!" said Amy. They looked at Tatiana, smiling.

"I may be going home this afternoon," Tatiana said.

"So what did you think?" asked Amy.

"About what?"

Nicola's eyes widened. "You got my note!"

"Well, I – I didn't read it. I wanted to tell you, but –"

"You didn't read it?"

"Oh, for goodness sake!" said Amy.

"I wanted to read it, but I knew you were angry and, well – I threw it away."

Nicola shook her head in disbelief. "You are something else, Tatiana Kumpf."

"So you don't know about the Science

Fair," said William.

"No." Tatiana tried to sound matter-of-fact. "I suppose you won, William."

"No, I told you I didn't expect to win. I got an honourable mention." He sat there, smiling.

"Who won, then?"

"*You* did!" they all said together.

"Me? I wasn't even in it."

"Yes you were," said Amy. "You'd better tell her, Nicola."

"I hardly know where to start." Nicola cleared her throat. "It was all in my note. Amy was the one who fixed the computer."

Amy? The words flowed over Tatiana.

"I had to reset it," Amy said, "and then go into the monitor and poke around a bit. My dad helped. Then when we found a memory location with something that looked like data, we saved it. It was a bit garbled, but Nicola made sense out of it. She pulled your notes back out of the waste-paper basket."

"You got it back?"

"Eventually. We were up half the night, mind you."

Tatiana stared at them. "You stayed up half the night and got it back?"

Amy shrugged. "Nicola wanted to," she said. "Friends are friends, even if they're mad at each other. Besides, it was a challenge to try and fix it."

Tatiana twisted the magazine tight in her hands.

"I was really careful the second time," Nicola said. "I felt awful. I was so tired I could hardly see the keys, but Amy kept me going. She insisted we mustn't give up."

Amy continued. "Yes, well, then when we phoned in the morning, your mum told us what happened."

"But how could I win if I wasn't there?"

"We were going, anyway," said William. "It wasn't any trouble putting your posters and stuff in the car. It was all ready. It fitted in OK between the cabbages."

"You took it for me, William?" Tatiana couldn't imagine anything more generous.

"I set it up as good as I could," said Nicola. "You would have done better. And I explained things to the judges. I told them why you weren't there. They really liked your project. They said you'd made an excellent effort. They said you could have maybe mentioned humidity or something. But they liked the photos, and the way you used science to prove something."

The truth was sinking in. "I won! I won the Science Fair! Whoopee!" Tatiana hurled the magazine across the room.

"You did it," Nicola said, laughing. "We didn't add anything."

"I won the Science Fair, and I didn't even know I was in it!" Tatiana stopped suddenly. "But why didn't Mum and Dad tell me?"

"They said it was our surprise," Amy said. "They wanted us to tell you."

Tatiana looked at her friends. Nicola, her soft oval face framed by long blonde hair. Amy, leaning forward in her wheelchair, her eyes bright. William, balancing a hospital menu on his head.

"You did all that for me?" Tatiana's voice was husky. "Thanks," she said quietly. "You're the best friends anyone could ever have."

The air conditioner hummed, and on the loudspeaker another doctor was being paged.

"Another time I'll start earlier," Tatiana said.

The others looked at each other.

"I will, too. You'll see." She knew they did not believe her, but that was OK. Now she knew she could finish things. Now she wasn't a quitter any more. Tatiana Alexandra Kumpf could do great things. Watch out, world!

"They loved William's jack-o'-lantern," Amy said. "You should have heard them giggling about it. But only one of the judges tried his cabbage pie."

"They told me I should have narrowed my focus a bit," said William, "and put in more science. They were right, too. And my display was not too neat. But they said it was creative. The cabbage juice must have got to them."

"I won the Science Fair!" Tatiana said softly. "I've never won anything in my whole life!"

"Sure you won, Tatty. You worked hard for it. We knew you could, if you'd just stick with it for a change." William's blue eyes twinkled. He didn't seem one bit jealous.

"I couldn't have done it without all of you," Tatiana said simply.

A nurse came in to check Tatiana's dressings. She smiled at Amy watching from her wheelchair. "And how are you doing?"

"I'm fine," replied Amy, evenly.

Tatiana was so used to Amy now that she hardly saw the wheelchair. But other people noticed it before anything else.

How did I know there was a log there that wasn't there the year before? Tatiana remembered that black icy road, and understood.

"We gotta go," said William. "My dad drove us, and he's waiting."

"Hold on a minute, William!" Tatiana struggled to say it. "I – you can call me Tatty if you like."

William grinned. "All right!" he said. "Race you to the elevator, Amy."

They disappeared down the hall.

Nicola hung back. "I brought a get-well present for you." From a bag she pulled a pink and silver parcel, topped with a shimmery bow.

Inside was a book. *Women of Science: Twenty-five Women Who Made a Difference.*

"Thanks!" said Tatiana. "You really know what I like."

"They had some great posters," Nicola said, "but I knew you'd like this better. Oh, hello!"

Mum and Dad were at the door.

"Congratulations! You did it!" Dad smiled that crinkled smile. "We were bursting to tell you."

Mum did a series of pirouettes across Tatiana's room. Her bag banged against her arm and her coat flapped.

"Lorraine!" Dad said, laughing.

Nicola clapped. "That's pretty good, Mrs Kumpf."

Mum danced back to them and hugged each of the girls in turn. "Tatiana, I'm so proud of you. I was telling Ida all about it. Just think, twenty-five pounds, plus helping at the University this summer. We knew you could do it, didn't we, Nicola?"

Nicola nodded.

"You just have to not give up," said Tatiana. "Like Amy. Not ever let anything stop you."

"And let people help you sometimes," said Nicola.

Mum noticed the book. "Look at this, Peter. What a thoughtful girl you are, Nicola."

"Yes, she is," Tatiana said.

After Nicola left, Mum tucked Tatiana in again. "You rest before lunch," she said. "Then when the doctor comes, you'll probably be able to go home."

Tatiana looked drowsily towards the window. Tree branches dripped and glistened in the sunshine. Spring was on its way.

"Mum?"

Tatiana had always had trouble saying important things, she knew that. But today she'd begun to learn. She looked at Mum and Dad, smiling down at her from each side of the bed.

"Mum?" It would sound foolish, but she said it anyway. "Do you like me?"

"Like you?" Mum's eyes widened. "Of course we like you. We love you. You know that."

"Just the way I am?"

"Just the way you are."

Tatiana looked at Mum, at the soft brown curls framing her pretty face. She turned and looked at Dad.

He nodded. "Yes, just the way you are. And some day you'll be a scientist, if that's what you want. Move over, Einstein."

Tatiana grinned. She felt worn out, but

for the first time in ages she also felt at peace with herself. "It'll be good to get home," she said.

She missed the flat, she missed Mum's cooking, she missed Dad thumping his foot at the television. "It'll be good to get home," she said again.

Tatty Kumpf, Scientist. It wasn't such a bad name after all.

READ MORE IN PUFFIN

For children of all ages, Puffin represents quality and variety – the very best in publishing today around the world.

For complete information about books available from Puffin – and Penguin – and how to order them, contact us at the appropriate address below. Please note that for copyright reasons the selection of books varies from country to country.

On the worldwide web: www.puffin.co.uk

In the United Kingdom: Please write to *Dept. EP, Penguin Books Ltd, Bath Road, Harmondsworth, West Drayton, Middlesex UB7 0DA*

In the United States: Please write to *Consumer Sales, Penguin USA, P.O. Box 999, Dept. 17109, Bergenfield, New Jersey 07621-0120*. VISA and MasterCard holders call 1-800-253-6476 to order Penguin titles

In Canada: Please write to *Penguin Books Canada Ltd, 10 Alcorn Avenue, Suite 300, Toronto, Ontario M4V 3B2*

In Australia: Please write to *Penguin Books Australia Ltd, P.O. Box 257, Ringwood, Victoria 3134*

In New Zealand: Please write to *Penguin Books (NZ) Ltd, Private Bag 102902, North Shore Mail Centre, Auckland 10*

In India: Please write to *Penguin Books India Pvt Ltd, 706 Eros Apartments, 56 Nehru Place, New Delhi 110 019*

In the Netherlands: Please write to *Penguin Books Netherlands bv, Postbus 3507, NL-1001 AH Amsterdam*

In Germany: Please write to *Penguin Books Deutschland GmbH, Metzlerstrasse 26, 60594 Frankfurt am Main*

In Spain: Please write to *Penguin Books S. A., Bravo Murillo 19, 1° B, 28015 Madrid*

In Italy: Please write to *Penguin Italia s.r.l., Via Felice Casati 20, I-20124 Milano*

In France: Please write to *Penguin France S. A., 17 rue Lejeune, F-31000 Toulouse*

In Japan: Please write to *Penguin Books Japan, Ishikiribashi Building, 2-5-4, Suido, Bunkyo-ku, Tokyo 112*

In South Africa: Please write to *Longman Penguin Southern Africa (Pty) Ltd, Private Bag X08, Bertsham 2013*